The Birthday Pet

by Ellen Javernick

illustrated by Kevin O'Malley

Marshall Cavendish Children

Box turtles are challenging pets to own. They require specially designed pens and a varied diet. In addition, they can carry Salmonella, so hygiene is important when handling them and cleaning their pens. This story was inspired by a child who took excellent care of his pet box turtle.

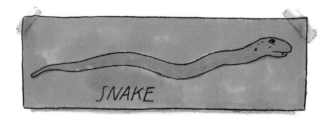

Marshall Cavendish Corporation, 99 White Plains Road, Tarrytown, NY 10591
www.marshallcavendish.us/kids

Library of Congress Cataloging-in-Publication Data
Javernick, Ellen.
The birthday pet / by Ellen Javernick ; illustrated by Kevin O'Malley.
p. cm.
Summary: Danny can have a pet for his birthday and he knows exactly what he wants, but the other members of his family think differently.
ISBN 978-0-7614-5522-6
[1. Stories in rhyme. 2. Pets—Fiction. 3. Turtles—Fiction. 4. Birthdays—Fiction.] I. O'Malley, Kevin, 1961- ill. II. Title.
PZ8.3.J36Bi 2009
[E]—dc22
2008010740

The illustrations are rendered in design markers and colored pencil.
Book design by Anahid Hamparian
Editor: Margery Cuyler

Printed in Malaysia
First edition
1 3 5 6 4 2

Marshall Cavendish
Children

To the boys and girls from both Garfield and
Namaqua Elementary Schools
—E.J.

2, 4, 6, 8, who do I appreciate...
Anahid Hamparian,
Sensationnel Directeur Artistique
—K.O.

It was Danny's birthday,
and his folks said he could get
any kind of animal
he wanted for a pet.

Danny thought it over
before he went to bed.
"All I really want
is a turtle," he said.

But instead . . .
Dad said,
"You don't want a pet
that sits still like a log.
So he went out and got Danny a . . .

. . . dog.

The dog knocked Danny over
when they went outside to play.
If Danny took her walking,
she always ran away.

"How's the dog?" asked his father.
Danny shook his head.
"All I really want
is a turtle," he said.

But instead . . .
Mom said,
"A turtle's not cuddly
or soft like a mitten.
So she went out and got Danny a . . .

. . . kitten.

The kitten was cuddly,
but it made Danny sneeze,
and he always had to get it
down from the trees.

"How's the kitten?" asked his mother.
Danny shook his head.
"All I really want
is a turtle," he said.

But instead . . .
his big brother said,
"You ought to pick a pet
more exciting than that.
So he went out and got Danny a . . .

. . . rat.

The rat's beady eyes
were a scary sight,
and the rat kept Danny up
when it gnawed in the night.

"How's the rat?" asked his brother.
Danny shook his head.
"All I really want
is a turtle," he said.

But instead . . .
his older sister said,
"You would like a turtle?
A turtle is absurd."
So she went out and got Danny a . . .

. . . bird.

The bird only nipped.
It didn't even talk.
It was sort of pretty,
but it had a nasty squawk.

"How's the bird?" asked his sister.
Danny shook his head.
"Not one of you listened
to anything I said!"

So instead . . .
his family got Danny a . . .

turtle . . .

with a nice hard shell.
Danny couldn't wait
for his show-and-tell.

The turtle blinked her eyes
and never made a sound.

She played peekaboo,
as she crawled around.

He fed her bugs and lettuce,
and he made a turtle gym.

Danny thought the turtle
was the perfect pet for him.

So Dad kept the dog,
his brother kept the rat,

his sister kept the bird,
and Mom kept the cat.

Danny kept the turtle,
and that was the end of that!